JAN THOMAS

Beach Lane Books
New York   London   Toronto   Sydney   New Delhi

For Teri!

BEACH LANE BOOKS

An imprint of Simon & Schuster Children's Publishing Division

1230 Avenue of the Americas, New York, New York 10020

© 2022 by Jan Thomas

Book design by Rebecca Syracuse © 2022 by Simon & Schuster, Inc.

BEACH LANE BOOKS and colophon are trademarks of Simon & Schuster, Inc.

For information about special discounts for bulk purchases, please contact Simon & Schuster Special Sales at 1-866-506-1949 or business@simonandschuster.com.

The Simon & Schuster Speakers Bureau can bring authors to your live event. For more information or to book an event, contact the Simon & Schuster Speakers Bureau at 1-866-248-3049 or visit our website at www.simonspeakers.com.

The text for this book was set in Chaloops.

The illustrations for this book were rendered digitally.

Manufactured in China

1021 SCP

First Edition

2 4 6 8 10 9 7 5 3 1

Library of Congress Cataloging-in-Publication Data

Names: Thomas, Jan, 1958– author.

Title: Even robots aren't perfect! / Jan Thomas.

Description: First edition. | New York : Beach Lane Books, 2022. | Audience: Ages 0-8 | Audience: Grades 2-3 | Summary: In three stories, best friends Red Robot and Blue Robot learn about how sometimes they can make mistakes or say the wrong things yet still be friends with each other.

Identifiers: LCCN 2021022427 (print) | LCCN 2021022428 (ebook) | ISBN 9781665911658 (hardcover) | ISBN 9781665911665 (ebook)

Subjects: CYAC: Friendship—Fiction. | Robots—Fiction. | Humorous stories.

Classification: LCC PZ7.T36694 Ev 2022 (print) | LCC PZ7.T36694 (ebook) | DDC [E]—dc23

LC record available at https://lccn.loc.gov/2021022427

LC ebook record available at https://lccn.loc.gov/2021022428

CONTENTS

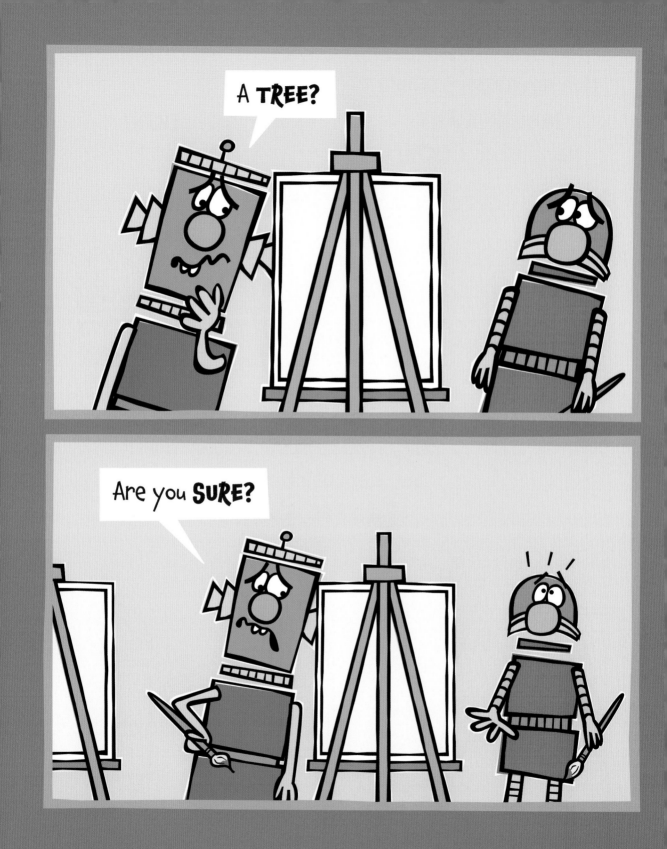

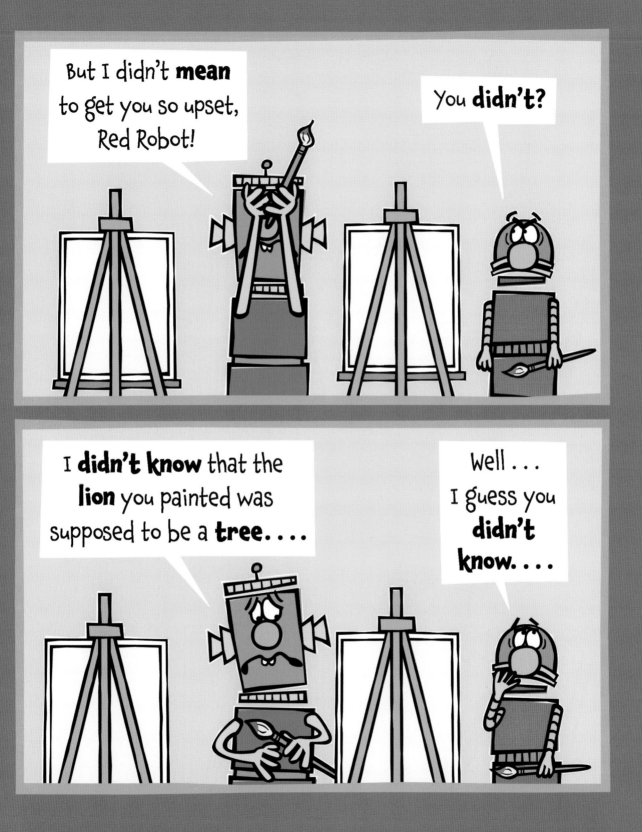

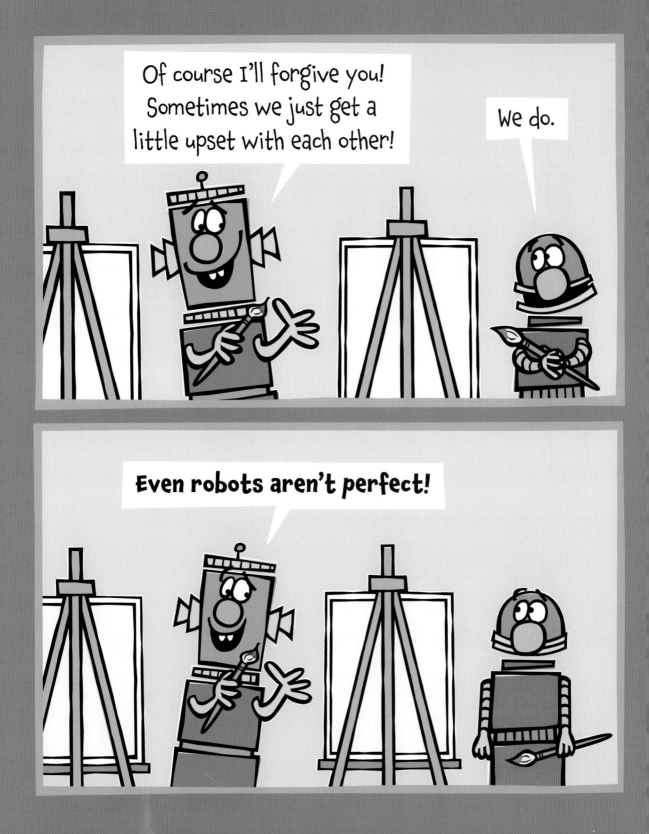

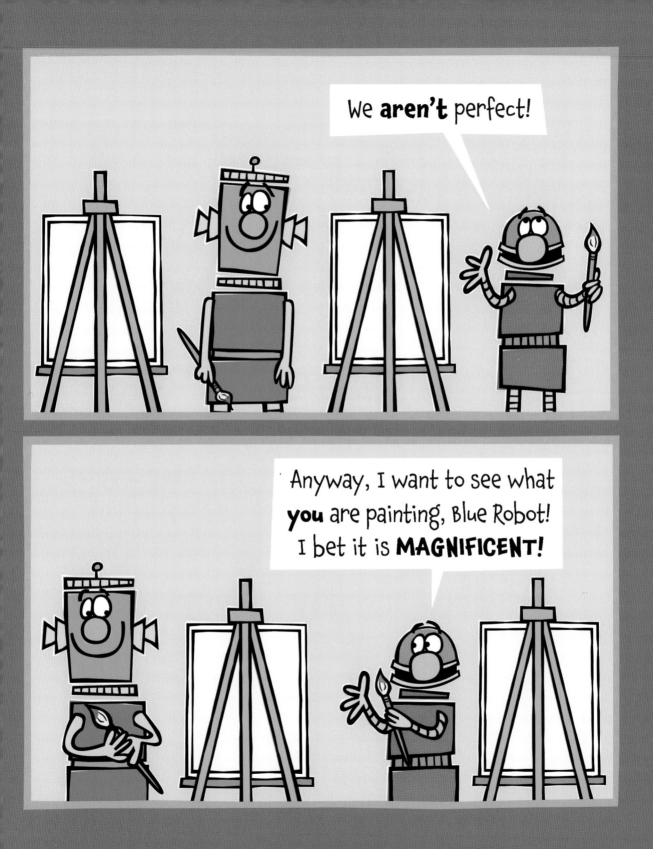

Oh dear! I just got upset! I'm SORRY I got upset!
I guess you didn't know that I painted a gnat wearing a green jacket and a funny hat.
No . . . I didn't know that. . . .

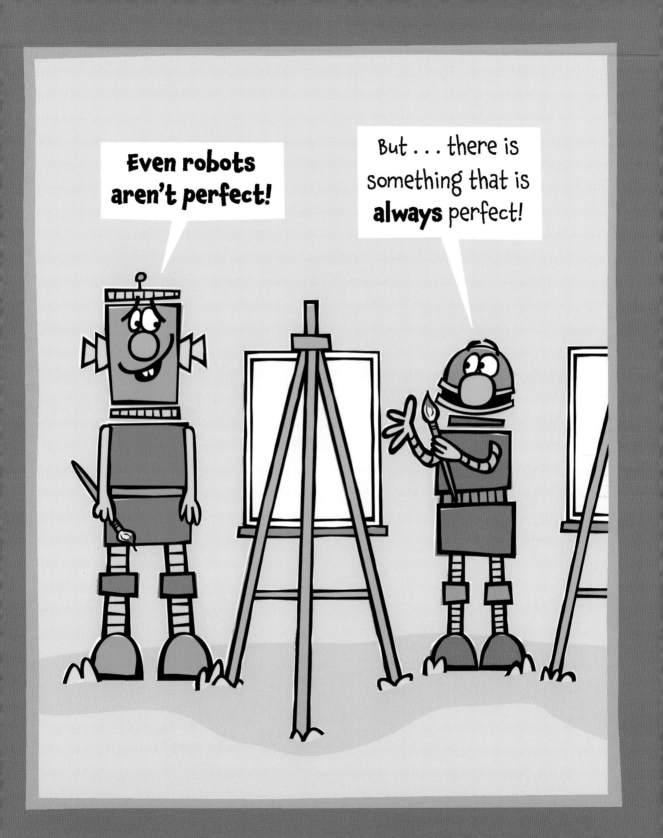

NOBODY LIKES
TO RUST

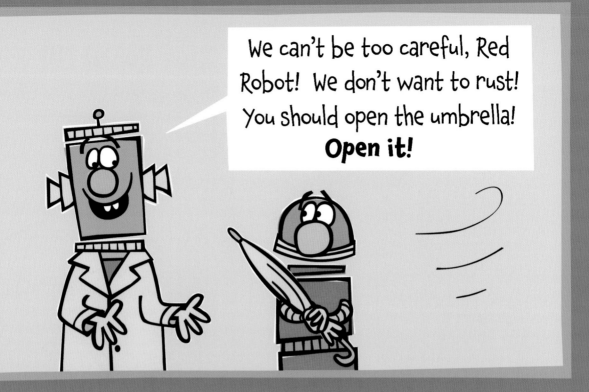

Well, no. My mind is **still** on the fact that I'm **FLYING AWAY,** Blue Robot.

Oh, Red Robot! I'm **sorry** I told you to open your umbrella!!! I didn't **MEAN** to make you fly away!!!

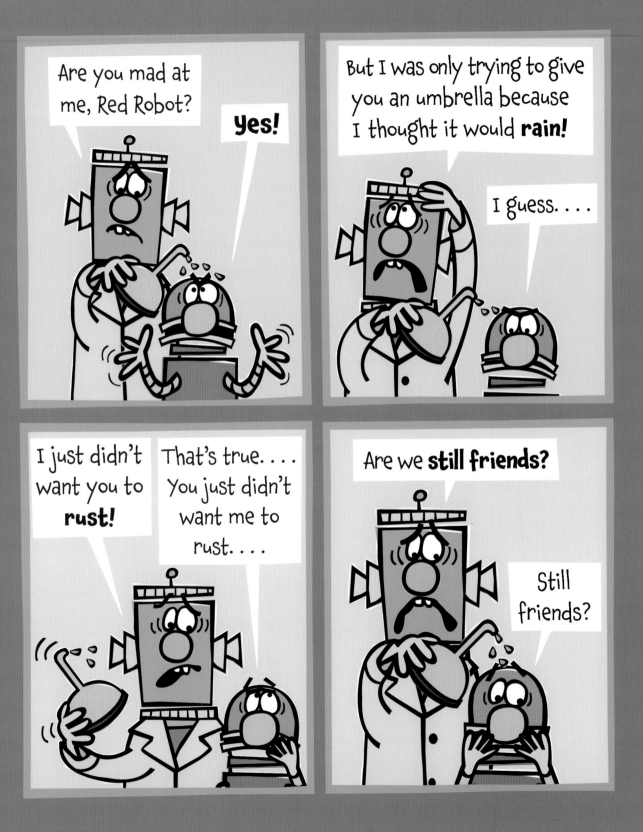

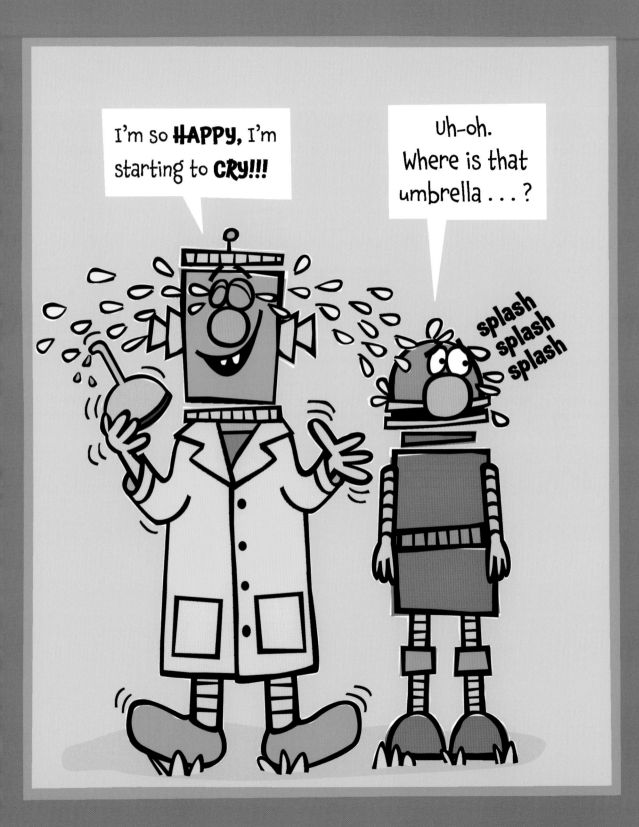

THE PERFECT PLAN

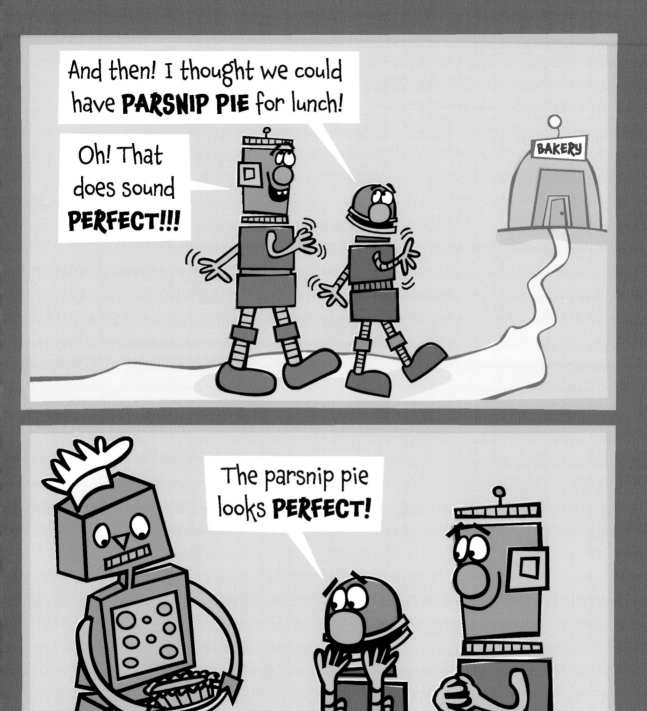

Uh...was that part of your perfect plan, Red Robot?

No.

A lot happened that was **not** part of my perfect plan, Blue Robot....

Really? But I **LOVED** your perfect plan!

Well, except for the last part....

Well, I'll **try** to be flexible. . . .